The Mag₁ ⸻ₒ
and other Russian Folktales

The Magic Ring

and other Russian Folktales

retold by Robert Chandler

illustrated by Ken Kiff

FABER & FABER
London · Boston

First published in 1979
by Faber and Faber Limited
3 Queen Square London WC1
Printed in Great Britain by
Butler & Tanner Ltd, Frome and London

British Library Cataloguing in Publication Data

Chandler, Robert
  The magic ring, and other Russian folktales.
  I. Kiff, Ken
  823'.9'1J   PZ8.1

ISBN 0-571-11338-9
ISBN 0-571-11338-9
ISBN 0-571-13006-2 *Pbk*

Contents

❦❦❦❦❦❦❦❦❦❦❦❦❦❦❦❦❦❦❦

Elyena the Wise and Ivan the Half-Wit

Once, a long time ago, there was an old peasant woman. She was a widow and she lived in a village with her son Ivan.

Time passed and Ivan became a man. His mother was very glad he was grown up now, but she did wish he wasn't such a half-wit. Whatever he did, he didn't seem to be able to put a foot right. Once he went out to plough. His mother said to him:

"Plough a bit deeper this time, son. The soil on top's been worn out."

Ivan ploughed as deep as he could, cutting right down into the clay and turning it up on top. Then he sowed the corn. It was all wasted.

It was the same with everything else. His mother grew very worried about him. She was old now and she couldn't work any longer. Soon they wouldn't have anything left to eat.

One day they ate their last crumb of bread. The mother began thinking again about her poor, half-wit son. She'd have to get someone to marry him. With a sensible wife even he might learn to do some real work and earn his keep for a change. But then who could she find? Not even a widow would want him for a husband.

Meanwhile, Ivan was just sitting outside, not thinking of anything in particular. Suddenly he looked up and saw an old man, a frail old man with moss on his clothes and a worn, pock-marked face that had been eaten away by the wind.

"Give us a bite to eat, son," said the old man. "I'm worn out from the road and I've eaten the last crumb in my bag."

"Grandfather, we ate our last crust yesterday. We didn't know you were coming or we'd have saved it for you. But come along in. I'll stoke up the bath-house for you and I'll wash your shirt."

Ivan heated up the bath-house, washed the dirt off the old man, beat him with a besom—a little brush made from birch twigs—so he'd work up a good sweat, cleaned his shirt and trousers and laid out a bed for him in the hut.

The old man slept well that night. When he woke up in the morning, he said:

"Thank you. I'll remember your kindness. If you're ever in trouble, just go into the forest. When you come to where the path forks, you'll find an old grey stone. Give it a push with your shoulder and call 'Grandfather'. I'll be there."

With that he went off.

Ivan and his mother really were in trouble. There was nothing to eat at all.

"You wait here," said Ivan. "I'll go and fetch some bread."

"Oh yes!" she answered. "Where's a half-wit like you going to find bread? Get some for yourself if you can, but don't worry about me. I'll die as I am. Find yourself a good wife now. Then you won't go hungry again."

Ivan sighed and went off to the forest. He came to the place where the path forked and pushed the stone.

"Is something the matter?" said the old man. "Or have you just come on a visit?"

8

They walked deeper into the forest till they came to some fine huts. The old man took Ivan straight into the biggest of them. Ivan could see who was the master here.

The old man called his cook and his servant and said they'd like some roast sheep to start off with. When it was ready, he served Ivan himself. Ivan ate everything off his plate and asked for more.

"Tell them to roast another sheep and bring me a good thick hunk of bread."

The old man told his servants to roast another sheep and bring in a whole loaf of fresh wheaten bread.

"There you are," he said. "Eat as much as you've room for. Or do you want to keep it for later?"

"Thank you," said Ivan. "I've had all I want myself. Ask your servant to take the sheep and the bread to my mother. She's got nothing to eat at all."

The old man told his servants to take a whole sheep and two loaves of white bread to Ivan's mother. Then he asked:

"How come you and your mother haven't got any food? You're a man now. Soon you'll be getting married. How are you going to keep your family then?"

"I don't know, Grandfather," said Ivan. "Anyway, I have no sweetheart."

"That's not right," said the old man. "Why don't you marry my daughter then? She's got enough wit for you both."

He called his daughter. A beautiful young girl came in. No one had ever seen such beauty or even known it could be found in the world. Ivan couldn't take his eyes off her.

The father looked severely at his daughter and said:

"This is your husband. Be a good wife to him."

His beautiful daughter looked modestly down at the floor.

"As you wish, Father."

Soon they were married and living together. They lived well and had everything they needed. Ivan's wife ran the house herself as her father was nearly always away. He was travelling in distant countries, searching for wisdom. Whenever he found some, he came back home and wrote it down in his book.

Once he came back with a little round mirror. It was a magic mirror. He'd bought it from a craftsman-magician far away in the Cold Mountains. He hid it away without showing it to anyone.

Ivan's mother was very well now and she had plenty to eat. She still lived in her old hut in the village. Her son kept asking her to come and live with him and his wife, but she always refused. She didn't like the idea of living with her daughter-in-law.

"I don't know what," she said, "but there's something wrong. Your wife's too rich and too beautiful. What have you done to deserve her? Your father and I were poor enough and you were born with a wooden ladle in your mouth."

She stayed in her old hut. Ivan thought about what she'd said. It was true. His wife was very sweet to him and she always did what he told her. Life went on very smoothly. Deep inside, though, he always felt cold.

One day the old man came in and said to Ivan:

"I'm going a long way away, further than I've ever been before. I won't be back for a long time. Now I want you to look after this key for me. I used to take it myself but this time I'm afraid of losing it. Take good care of it, and whatever you do, don't open the barn door with it. And if you do go into the barn, don't take your wife. And if you do take your wife, don't give her the coloured dress that hangs there. I'll give it to her myself, but not till the right time. Well, take care. Remember my words or you'll make your life into death."

With that he went away.

After a few days Ivan couldn't help thinking:

"No, it won't do any harm if I just go in and have a look. I won't take Elyena."

Ivan went up to the barn that had always been kept locked. He opened it and went in. There were great heaps of gold ingots and there were stones that flamed like fire. There were many other wonders that Ivan didn't even know the name of. And in the corner there was a little door.

Ivan opened it. Before he'd even taken a step, he shouted out:

"Elyenushka! Quick! Come here!"

There was a beautiful dress in this little room. It shone like a clear sky and the light flowed over it like wind. Ivan was very happy. He couldn't wait to show it to Elyena. He knew it would suit her and that it was just the right size.

For a moment he half-remembered the old man's words but then he forgot them again. After all, he was only going to show her the dress.

Elyena came in. She saw the dress and flung up her arms in amazement.

"Oh!" she said. "What a dress!"

And then:

"Quick! Help me into it. You can tie the laces for me."

Ivan told her that was forbidden. She began to cry.

"So that's how much you love me," she said. "You won't even give me a nice dress. You might at least let me slip my arms through the sleeves to see how it feels. Maybe it won't be right."

Ivan gave his permission.

His wife slipped her arms through the sleeves. Then she asked again:

"I can't see anything. Let me just put my head through the collar."

Ivan gave his permission. She put her head through the collar, pulled the dress down and smoothed it over. She felt a little mirror in one of the pockets, took it out and began to look at herself.

"My, what a beauty!" she cried out. "Why should I live with a half-wit husband? I should be a bird. Then I'd fly far, far away."

She flung up her arms and was gone. She was a dove and she was flying far, far away into the blue sky, wherever she wished. The dress she'd put on was a magic one.

Ivan could hardly believe his eyes. He hadn't got time to feel sorry for himself though. He put some bread in his knapsack and set off to search for his wife.

"The bad girl!" he said. "Going off like that without a word. Disobeying her father and leaving his house. I'll knock some sense into her head."

Then Ivan remembered he was only a half-wit himself and began to cry.

He walked along roads, along tracks, along paths. He walked where there were no paths at all. It was hard going and he was feeling down-hearted. Suddenly he saw a pike lying beside a stream. It was dying and it couldn't get back into the water.

"Well," he said, "I may be down on my luck but he's even worse off."

He picked the pike up and put it back in the water. It dived deep down, shot up again, stuck its head out of the water and said:

"I won't forget your kindness. When things are bad, just say: 'Pike, pike, remember Ivan!'"

Ivan stopped to eat a piece of bread and went on again. He'd walked a long way. It was almost night.

He looked up and saw a little sparrow. A kite had seized it in its talons and was about to eat it.

"I may be in a bad way myself," said Ivan, "but that sparrow's about to die."

Ivan scared the kite away. It dropped the sparrow.

The sparrow perched on a branch and said:

"When you need me, just call out: 'Ey! Sparrow! remember my kindness!' "

Ivan spent the night under a tree and set off again next morning. He'd come a long way from home and he was tired. He'd got so thin he had to hold up his trousers to keep them from falling. He still had a long way to go though. He walked on for another year and another six months. Then he came to the ocean. He'd crossed the whole world and there was nowhere further to go.

He asked someone who lived there:

"What land is this? Who are the Tsar and Tsaritsa here?"

The man answered:

"Elyena the Wise is Tsaritsa here. She knows everything. She's got a book with everything written down in it and a magic mirror where she can see everything in the world. She can probably even see you right now."

He was right. Elyena had seen Ivan in her mirror. Her maid Darya had wiped the mirror clean and then looked into it to see how beautiful she was. Instead she'd caught sight of Ivan.

"Look!" she said. "There's a stranger outside. He must have come a long way. He's all thin and worn out and his sandals are torn to ribbons."

Elyena the Wise looked in the mirror herself.

"That's no stranger!" she said. "That's my own husband."

Ivan went up to the palace. It was surrounded by a wooden fence. On each stake hung a man's skull. There was just one stake that didn't have anything on it.

Ivan went up to someone and asked him the meaning of all this.

"Those are the suitors of our Tsaritsa. You've never seen anyone like our Tsaritsa. She's more beautiful than words can tell and she's an enchantress. Brave, noble suitors keep coming and asking for her hand but she refuses them all. She won't accept anyone unless he can outwit her. If a suitor fails to outwit her, she has him executed and puts his head on a stake. Now there's only one stake left. That'll be for the next man who wants to marry her."

"I'm going to marry her," said Ivan.

"Then it'll be your head on that stake," said the man and went back into his hut.

Ivan walked into the palace. Elyena was sitting in her chamber, wearing her magic dress.

"What do you think you're doing here?" she asked.

"I wanted to see you again," he answered. "I missed you."

"Other people have missed me too," she said, pointing to the heads outside.

"Aren't you a wife to me any more then?"

"I was once," said the Tsaritsa, "but I've changed. How can a peasant like you be my husband? If you want me, you must win me again. And if you fail, I'll have your head chopped off. Your stake's waiting outside."

"Oh no, it isn't," said Ivan. "You watch what you say. Anyway, what do you want me to do?"

"You must hide yourself away where I can't find you, or so I can't recognize you if I do. You can try anywhere under the sun. If you outwit me, you can marry me. If you fail, you lose your head."

"Let me eat your bread and sleep on your straw. I'll do what you say in the morning."

That evening Darya laid out some straw for Ivan and brought him some bread and a jug of kvass. He had something to eat, lay down and began wondering what the morning would bring.

After a while Darya came back. She sat down, spread out the magic dress and started to darn a hole in it. She sewed

14

and sewed, as carefully as she possibly could. Then she began to cry.

"What's the matter, Darya?" asked Ivan.

"I'm going to die tomorrow," she said. "The Tsaritsa told me to darn her dress, but the cloth's so delicate it just tears. I can't do anything with it at all. And if I don't finish it, the Tsaritsa will have me executed."

"Let me try," said Ivan. "Maybe I'll be able to do it and you won't have to die."

"A fat lot you'll be able to do," she answered. "The Tsaritsa called you a half-wit. Still, you may as well try. I'll watch."

Ivan got up, took the dress and began sewing. The dress just tore even more. It was as light as air and there was nowhere for the needle to take hold. Ivan threw the needle away and began tying the threads with his fingers.

Darya was furious.

"You idiot! What on earth do you think you're doing? There are hundreds and thousands of threads there. How can you tie them all with your fingers?"

"Where there's a will, there's a way. But don't worry. You can go to bed now. I'll be finished by morning."

Ivan worked all night. There was a moon and anyway the dress shone by itself. He could see every thread.

He finished a little before dawn and stopped to look at his work. The hole had gone and the cloth felt quite smooth. He picked the dress up. It seemed heavy. He turned it over and found a book in one of the pockets. It was the one Elyena's father had written down all his wisdom in. In the other pocket lay the round mirror he had brought back from the crafts-man-magician in the Cold Mountains. Ivan looked into it, but it was so cloudy he couldn't see anything. Then he looked at the book and couldn't understand a word. "I suppose it's true," he thought, "I really must be a half-wit."

15

Darya came in next morning, picked the dress up, looked it over and said:

"Thank you. You've saved me from death. I won't forget your kindness."

Then the sun rose. It was time for Ivan to go and hide. He went out into the yard and climbed into a haystack. He thought he'd be safe there but his legs were sticking out. All the dogs in the yard began barking at him and Darya shouted:

"Get out of there, you half-wit. You can't even hide from me, let alone from the Tsaritsa. And don't put mud all over the hay either."

Ivan climbed out of the haystack and wondered where to go next. Then he caught sight of the sea. He remembered the pike and wandered down to the shore.

"Pike! Pike!" he said. "Remember Ivan!"

The pike was there in the twinkling of an eye.

"Quick!" he said. "I'll hide you at the bottom of the ocean."

Ivan dived in. The pike pulled him down to the bottom, buried him deep in the sand and stirred up the water with his tail.

Elyena the Wise took her magic mirror and held it to the earth. Ivan wasn't there. She held it to the sky. Ivan wasn't there either. She held it to the ocean. All she could see was muddy water. "I may be Elyena the Wise," she thought, "but Ivan the Half-wit's nobody's fool."

She opened her Book of Wisdom and read: "Cunning is powerful but kindness is stronger still. Even a beast remembers kindness." Then she looked at the page again. This time she saw other words. She read: "Ivan lies buried in the sand at the bottom of the ocean. Call the pike and tell him to fetch Ivan. Say that if he doesn't, you'll have him fried for dinner."

Elyena sent her maid Darya to call the pike and tell him to fetch Ivan.

Soon Ivan appeared before Elyena the Wise a second time.

"Have me executed," he said. "I'm not worthy of you."

But Elyena the Wise decided to let him off. She could always have him executed later and, after all, it wasn't as though they were strangers.

"Go and hide again. If you outwit me this time, I'll pardon you. If you fail, I'll have you executed."

Ivan set off to find a place where he'd be safe from the Tsaritsa. He didn't know what to do. Elyena could see everything in the world in her magic mirror. If there was anything she couldn't see, she could read about it in her book.

Ivan called out:

"Ey! Sparrow! Remember my kindness!"

And there was the sparrow.

"Fall down on the ground," he said. "Be a grain of wheat."

Ivan fell down and turned into a grain of wheat. The sparrow pecked him up in his beak.

Elyena the Wise turned her mirror to the earth, then to the sky, then to the seas. She could see everything except what she wanted. She lost her temper and smashed the mirror to pieces against the floor. Then Darya slipped in and carried the pieces away in the hem of her skirt.

Elyena the Wise opened her father's book. In it she read: "Ivan is in the grain; the grain is in the sparrow; the sparrow is on the fence."

Elyena sent Darya to call the sparrow and tell him he'd be fed to the kite unless he surrendered the grain.

The sparrow was very frightened. He dropped the grain as quick as he could. It fell on the ground and there was Ivan.

Ivan was brought before Elyena the Wise a third time.

"Execute me," he said. "It's true: you're Elyena the Wise and I'm just a half-wit."

"Tomorrow," she answered. "Tomorrow I'll have your head stuck up on the last stake."

Ivan lay awake that evening, wondering what it would be like to die tomorrow. Then he thought of his mother. He loved her so much that he felt happy again straight away.

After a while Darya came in and brought him a bowl of porridge. He ate it hungrily and then thanked her. She looked at him for a moment and said:

"Don't you be frightened of our Tsaritsa, Ivan. She's not really as cruel as all that."

"A man doesn't fear his wife," said Ivan. "It's just that I want to knock some sense into her head."

"Don't be in too much of a hurry tomorrow," said Darya. "Say you want to see your mother and that you aren't yet ready to die."

Next morning Ivan said to Elyena:

"Let me live a little longer. I want to see my mother. She'll be here in a few days."

The Tsaritsa looked him over.

"I can't pardon you just like that," she said. "You must hide from me again. If I don't find you, you can live."

Ivan went off to find somewhere to hide. Darya went out after him.

"Wait a moment," she said. "I'll hide you this time. I haven't forgotten what you did for me."

She breathed on Ivan's face and he became a breath. She drew him into her chest. Then she went into the Tsaritsa's chamber and took her Book of Wisdom from off the table. She wiped the dust off it, opened it and breathed on it. Her breath became a letter. Ivan was the new first letter of the book's title.

A few minutes later Elyena the Wise came in and looked in the book to see where Ivan was hiding. The book didn't say anything, or if it did, the Tsaritsa couldn't make head or tail of it. She didn't know that the new letter had changed the meaning of every word.

Elyena the Wise slammed the book shut and threw it on the floor.

The letters all dropped out. The new first letter turned back into Ivan.

Ivan looked at Elyena the Wise, his wife, and couldn't take his eyes off her. Elyena gazed at him too and she began to smile. She became even more beautiful than she'd been before.

"I thought I had a half-wit for a husband," she said, "but

he hid from the Magic Mirror and he outwitted the Book of Wisdom."

They lived happily together from that moment to the end of their days. One evening, though, a few months later, Elyena said to Ivan:

"Why hasn't your mother come yet?"

"I don't know. We haven't seen your father for a long time either. I'll set out tomorrow and look for them."

Ivan's mother and Elyena's father were with their children again before daybreak. Elyena's father knew a short cut to her kingdom. They'd got there in no time at all and weren't even the least bit tired.

Ivan bowed to his mother and then fell at the old man's feet.

"I'm sorry, Father. I broke my word. Forgive your half-wit son."

The old man put his arms round him and kissed him.

"Thank you, son," he said. "There was wisdom in the book and there was beauty in the dress. The magic mirror showed everything that was happening in the world. I thought they'd make a good dowry for my daughter but I didn't want to give them to her too soon. And I still hadn't brought the one gift that really matters. I went to search for it in distant countries but it was right under my nose all the time. It's not something you can buy or even be given—each man must find it himself."

Elyena the Wise began to cry. She kissed her husband Ivan and begged his forgiveness.

From then on they all lived together in Elyena's palace and as far as I know they're still there.

The Magic Ring

Once upon a time there was an old widow. She lived in a village with her son Semyon.

The two of them were very poor. They slept on straw at night, their clothes were all worn and patched and they had hardly a crumb to put in their mouths. All this was a long time ago when the peasants hardly had any land and what land they did have was almost barren. What the peasants managed to sow would be killed by the frosts. If it escaped the frosts, it would be destroyed by droughts or floods. If it escaped the droughts and floods, it would be eaten by locusts.

Semyon used to go into town once a month to collect his mother's pension of one kopeck.

Once, when he was on his way back, he saw someone strangling a dog with a piece of rope. It was a very small, white dog, just a puppy.

"Why not leave the poor animal alone?" said Semyon.

"It's my dog. I'll do what I like with it."

"Sell him to me for a kopeck."

"All right."

Semyon gave the man his one kopeck, picked up the puppy and set off back home.

When he got back, he said to his mother:

"I couldn't find a cow or a horse, but I've brought a puppy instead."

"You idiot!" she shouted. "We haven't got anything to eat ourselves. How can we feed a puppy?"

"Don't worry, Mother. Dogs are as good as cows. They just bark instead of mooing."

A month later Semyon went to town again for the pension. It had gone up. This time they gave him two kopecks.

On his way back he met the same man. This time he was torturing a cat.

Semyon ran up to him.

"Why are you torturing the poor cat?"

"Mind your own business. It's my cat. I'll do what I like with it."

"Sell it to me."

"All right. A cat costs more than a dog though."

They settled on two kopecks.

This time Semyon's mother was really furious. She scolded him all day and started again early next morning.

A month later Semyon went into town again. This time he was given three kopecks.

On his way back he found the strange man. Now he was strangling a snake.

"Don't kill her. I've never seen a snake like that before. She must be very rare. I'm sure she's not poisonous."

He bought the snake for three kopecks, which was all the money he had in the world. Then he set off back home, carrying the snake underneath his shirt.

Once the snake had got warm, she said to Semyon:

"You won't be sorry you spent all your money on me. I'm Skarapeya and I'm no ordinary snake. If it weren't for you,

I'd have died. My father will give you a handsome reward."

Semyon got back home and let the snake out from under his shirt. His mother climbed straight up onto the stove. She was tongue-tied with fright.

Now there were five of them, all living together—a white dog, a grey cat, Semyon, his mother, and Skarapeya the snake.

Things became a bit difficult. Semyon's mother and Skarapeya didn't get on together. The mother was always forgetting Skarapeya's food or not putting out her water. Sometimes she even stepped on her tail.

One day Skarapeya said to Semyon:

"Your mother doesn't know how to treat me. Take me back to my father."

The snake slid off along the ground. Semyon followed. He followed her a long time, day after day, night after night. They went deep into the forest. Semyon began to wonder where he was going and whether he would ever come back.

Skarapeya tried to cheer him up.

"Don't worry. There's not much further to crawl. We've already reached the border of the Kingdom of Snakes. Soon we'll meet my father, the Snake Tsar. Listen now. When I tell my father how you saved me, he'll thank you and offer you as much gold as you can take away. Refuse the gold and ask him to give you the ring he wears on his middle finger. It's a magic ring. My father's been keeping it for me, but I want you to have it."

Semyon and Skarapeya came to the palace of the Snake Tsar. The Tsar was very glad to see his daughter again.

He said to Semyon:

"Thank you, Semyon. You've saved my daughter. I'd give her to you in marriage but she's already betrothed. You must have as much gold as you wish."

Semyon refused. Instead he asked for the magic ring.

"Give me the ring you wear on your middle finger. It will be a keepsake to remember your daughter by. Yes, the one with the crushed snake's head and the two green stones that burn like eyes."

The Snake Tsar thought for a moment. Then he took off his ring and gave it to Semyon. At the same time he whispered in Semyon's ear and told him what he must do to summon the Magic Power.

Soon Semyon had to go. He said goodbye to the Tsar and his daughter. Then he said goodbye to the Tsar's adopted son, Aspid, who was standing nearby and looking at him enviously.

He went back to his mother's. The first night, as soon as his mother was in bed, he slipped his ring off his middle finger and onto his index finger. At once twelve young warriors appeared before him.

"Greetings, new master," they said. "What do you want done?"

"Put some flour in the barn, and some sugar, and a little butter."

"As you say, master!" said the warriors and vanished.

When he woke up next morning, Semyon saw his mother dipping dry crusts in water and chewing away at them with her few wobbly teeth.

"Let's have some pies for breakfast. Mix some dough."

"Are you mad, son? It's more than a year now since we last had some flour."

"Have a look in the barn, Mother. Maybe there's some in there."

"Why bother? Even the mice have all starved by now."

Still, she went along to have a look. She unfastened the bolt. The door swung open and she was almost buried by a great heap of flour.

After that they never went hungry again. Semyon sold half

the flour and bought lots of meat. They had rissoles for lunch every day. The cat and dog grew sleek and glossy.

One night Semyon saw a beautiful maiden in his sleep. When he woke up, she wasn't there any more. Semyon couldn't stop thinking of her but he didn't even know her father's name or where she lived.

Semyon slipped his ring from finger to finger.

"What are your orders?" asked the twelve warriors.

Semyon told them about his dream: he'd seen a beautiful maiden; he didn't know where she lived but he wanted to go there more than anything else in the world.

In the twinkling of an eye, Semyon was in the kingdom of this beautiful maiden.

He went up to someone and asked about her.

"Which one's that?" said the man.

Semyon told him all about her.

"That sounds like the Tsarevna."

Semyon called his warriors and asked to be taken into the palace. He saw the Tsarevna, the Tsar's daughter. She was even more beautiful than she'd been in his dream.

He gave a deep sigh—what else could he do?—and asked to be taken back home.

At home he felt sad and lonely. He longed for the Tsarevna. He could hardly eat his bread or drink his beer.

His mother began to worry.

"What's the matter with you, son? Are you ill or have you fallen in love?"

He told his mother everything. She was horrified.

"Whatever next? How can a peasant's son love a Tsarevna? Tsars are wicked, cunning people. The Tsar will laugh at you and play tricks on you. The one thing he won't do is give you his daughter. Marry a peasant's daughter if you want to be happy."

But Semyon would only say one thing:

26

"Go on, Mother, go and ask for the Tsarevna."

His mother refused to go. Semyon thought for a long time. Then he slipped the Snake's ring from finger to finger and called for his twelve warriors.

"What do you want, master?"

"I want a palace and I want it to be ready by morning. I want there to be a fine suite of rooms for my mother and a bed with a feather mattress."

"All right, master, we'll build your palace and we'll stuff your mother's mattress with the finest of feathers."

Semyon's mother sank so deep into her feather mattress that night that she could hardly get out of bed in the morning. She looked round her chamber and rubbed her eyes. She thought she was still dreaming.

Then Semyon came in and wished her good morning. She realized she must be awake.

"What's all this, son? Where's it all come from?"

"It came by itself. Now you'll be able to live in comfort and I'll be able to marry whoever I like."

His mother thought what a brave, clever son she had. Her son asked again:

"Go on, Mother. Now you really must go and ask for the Tsarevna."

The mother walked up and down the palace. She thought how rich and splendid everything looked.

"All right. We may not be their equals yet, but we're not far off it."

She set off.

In time she came to the Tsar's palace and walked straight into the Royal Chambers. The Tsar and Tsaritsa were drinking tea. They'd poured some of it into their saucers and were blowing on it to cool it down. The Tsarevna was looking through her dowry.

The Tsar and Tsaritsa carried on blowing into their

saucers. They didn't so much as look at Semyon's mother. Some of the tea splashed out onto the table-cloth. It was tea with sugar. A real Tsar, and he didn't even know how to drink tea.

Semyon's mother was very angry.

"That's tea, you know, not water. It's not for washing the table with."

The Tsar looked up.

"What are you doing here, Grandmother?"

Semyon's mother walked forward to the centre of the room.

"Good day, Tsar and Sovereign Emperor," she said. "We've got the money, you've got the goods. Allow my son to marry your daughter."

"Who is your son? Where are his estates and what is his lineage?"

"He's from a village a long way away and his father's a peasant. His name is Semyon Yegorovich. Do you know of him?"

The Tsar gaped in astonishment.

"Are you mad, woman? We've got so many suitors we don't know what to do with them. Do you think we'll let our daughter marry the son of a peasant?"

Semyon's mother took offence.

"My son's no ordinary peasant, thank you. He's worth more than the sons of ten Tsars. As for a mere daughter . . ."

The Tsar resorted to cunning.

"All right, tell your son to build a crystal bridge right from our palace to his front door. In the morning we'll ride over and take a look at his apartments."

Semyon's mother went back home. As she went in, she nearly tripped up over the cat and dog. They were so fat they could hardly move.

"A fat lot of use you are. Eating and sleeping all day. Why don't you go and catch rats?"

28

Then she told her son what had happened.

"I wasted my time, son. They didn't agree."

"What do you mean? Why not?"

"What did you expect, son? The Tsar just made fun of us. He wants you to build a crystal bridge between our palaces. Then he'll ride over and visit us."

"That's all right. That's child's play."

That night Semyon called his warriors and told them to build a crystal bridge all the way to the Tsar's palace. It was to be ready by morning.

Everywhere in the kingdom, from midnight till dawn, you could hear the ring of hammers and the rasping of saws.

In the morning Semyon went out to have a look. The bridge was finished and there was a beautiful carriage to ride across it in. It went all by itself without any horses.

"Come on, Mother. It's time you called the Tsar and Tsaritsa. Tell them I'll collect them in the carriage."

His mother set out.

She stepped onto the bridge, but the crystal was slippery and it was very windy. She sat down and slid all the way to the palace on her backside.

"Good morning," she said. "The bridge is finished. My son will be round to fetch you in about half an hour."

The Tsar put his head out of the window to have a look.

"Well," he said. "Who'd have thought it? Your son certainly knows a thing or two."

The Tsar put on his crown and his best brocade trousers. He called the Tsaritsa and went out to the bridge. First he tested the railings to see how firm they were. Then he ran his hand over the crystal to see if it was real.

Semyon drew up in his carriage. He leaped out and opened the door.

"Greetings, Sovereign Emperor and Empress. Be seated."

"With pleasure," said the Tsar. "My wife may be a little nervous though."

Semyon looked at the Tsaritsa. She threw up her hands in horror.

"I'm not going. It's awful. We'll just get thrown in the river."

The Tsar's courtiers came out. The eldest gave his advice.

"You must set an example, your highness. The people mustn't think you're afraid."

After that the Tsar didn't have much choice. He climbed into the carriage together with the Tsaritsa. The courtiers all crowded onto the footboards or hung from the door-handles.

The bell rang. The carriage whistled, hummed, roared and began to shake. It filled with clouds of steam, jumped forward and was off. It rocked from side to side all the way. It was a good thing there was only one bridge to cross.

Eventually they reached Semyon's house. Semyon jumped out to open the Tsar's door but the courtiers beat him to it. They lifted the Tsar and Tsaritsa out of the carriage and laid them on the ground. Then they began fanning them and holding smelling salts under their noses.

The Tsaritsa screamed and screamed. The Tsar didn't say a word. His face was quite white.

"My!" said the Tsaritsa. "I've never been so shaken about in my life. Where's that suitor gone? Quick; let him have the girl! We can go back on foot."

Everything went just as Semyon had wished. The Tsarevna was given to him in marriage and they began to live together. Everything seemed fine.

One day, though, something happened. Semyon and his wife had gone for a walk in the forest. They'd walked a very long way and then lain down under a tree for a rest.

Just then the Snake Tsar's adopted son, Aspid, happened to pass by. He saw the ring on Semyon's finger and went green with envy. First he began to hiss and then he turned into a viper. He'd been hankering after that ring for years and he'd kept asking the Snake Tsar to give it to him. The Snake Tsar had always refused and had never told him its secret.

Aspid turned himself into a beautiful maiden. He was even more beautiful than Semyon's wife. He woke Semyon, and began making signs to him. "I'll soon have that ring now," he thought.

Semyon looked at him for a moment and said:

"Be off with you. I don't care how beautiful you are. I love my wife and that's that. Go away."

Then he turned over and went back to sleep again.

Aspid turned himself into a handsome young prince. He woke up Semyon's wife and began strutting about in front of her.

"What a man!" thought the Tsarevna. "He's a thousand times more handsome than my husband. If only he'd been one of my suitors!"

Aspid came closer and held out his hand. The Tsarevna got up and then looked down at Semyon. There were bits of snot in his nostrils and they jumped about as he breathed.

"Who are you?" she asked Aspid.

"I'm the Tsar's son. They call me the Prince of Warriors."

"I'm the Tsar's daughter."

"Follow me then. I'll treat you as you deserve."

"All right. Let's go."

Aspid whispered something in the Tsarevna's ear. She nodded her head and Aspid went away by himself.

Semyon and the Tsarevna went back home together. She took him by the hand and asked if it was true he wore a magic ring. She said that if he really loved her, he'd have told her about it by now.

Semyon told her all about it and put the ring on her hand. He thought she loved him.

That night the Tsarevna called the twelve warriors.

"You called for us," they said. "What do you want, new mistress?"

"I want you to move my house and the crystal bridge. Take them to the Prince of Warriors."

Semyon Yegorovich had only been married a few weeks.

When he and his mother woke up, everything had gone. There was just an old hut and an empty barn. Semyon and his mother were alone again with the cat and the dog. There was nothing to eat.

Semyon didn't say a word. He hardly even sighed. He was thinking how his mother had told him never to marry a Tsarevna. He wished he'd listened.

He looked out of the window. The Tsar's carriage was approaching. Opposite the window it came to a stop and the Tsar got out. He looked round. There was no crystal bridge and no palace. All he could see was an old hut and Semyon looking out of the window.

"What's all this?" he shouted. "What have you done with my daughter? I'll teach you, you villain!"

Semyon went out and told the Tsar what had happened: he'd given the magic ring to his wife and she'd betrayed him.

The Tsar wouldn't believe him. He had him thrown into prison till he confessed what he'd done with his wife.

Semyon's mother was left on her own. There was nothing to eat in the house. She called the cat and the dog and set off to beg for food. She would beg for a crust underneath one window and eat it under the next. It was a hard life. The nights grew colder. Soon it would be winter.

One day the cat said to the dog:

"Soon we'll all be frozen to death. We must find the Tsarevna and get back the magic ring. Our master saved us from death. Now it's our turn to save him."

The dog agreed. He sniffed at the earth, paused for a moment and ran off. The cat followed.

They had a long way to go. It took them a long time, much longer than it takes to read this story.

They ran on and on till they came to the crystal bridge and the palace where they'd once lived with Semyon.

The dog waited outside while the cat stole in. She came to the room where Semyon's wife slept. She crept in. There was the ring. The Tsarevna was afraid of its being stolen and she kept it between her teeth. The cat could see it shining there.

The cat caught a mouse, gave him a friendly bite on the ear and told him what he must do to stay alive. The mouse climbed up onto the bed, crept quietly over the Tsarevna and tickled her in the nostril with his tail. The Tsarevna gave a big sneeze and her mouth fell open. The ring dropped onto the floor and rolled away.

The cat grabbed the ring and leaped out of the window. By the time the Tsarevna woke up, the ring was far away and the mouse was quietly gnawing a piece of old cheese in the kitchen.

The cat and the dog ran as fast as they could. They didn't even stop to eat or sleep. They ran over mountains, through forests, across fields. They swam over great lakes and rivers. All the way the cat kept the ring under her tongue and never once opened her mouth.

They came to the last river. They could already see Semyon's hut.

The dog said to the cat:

"You sit on my back. I'll swim. And whatever you do, don't open your mouth and drop the ring."

Half-way across, the dog said:

"Take care, puss. Don't say a word. You'll drop the ring."

The cat remained silent. Then again:

33

"Don't say anything, puss."

The cat still hadn't said a word. Again:

"Keep your mouth shut. Take care of the ring."

"But my mouth is shut," answered the cat and dropped the ring into the river.

As soon as they got to the bank, they started clawing and hissing and barking.

"It's all your fault, you stupid chatterbox of a cat."

"It's not. It's yours. You spoke first."

Just then some fishermen dragged in their net. They saw the cat and dog quarrelling and thought it was because they hadn't got anything to eat. They threw them some fish-guts.

The cat and dog caught the fish and started to eat. Suddenly there was a crunch. The cat had bitten something hard. She'd found the ring.

They forgot about the fish and ran back to the village. They looked inside the old hut but it was still empty. They ran on to the city and came to Semyon's prison.

The cat climbed up onto the outer wall and began to look for Semyon. She wanted to call him and miaow, but she was frightened of dropping the ring.

Towards evening Semyon looked out of his grating. He wanted to have a look at the world outside.

The cat was watching. She climbed down the wall, squeezed through the grating and jumped onto her master's shoulder.

"Well," thought Semyon, "you may only be a cat but at least your heart's in the right place."

The cat miaowed and dropped the ring on the floor.

Semyon picked it up and summoned his twelve warriors.

"Good day to you, old master. Say what you want done. We'll waste no time about it."

"Bring my old house back from wherever it is now. And if there's anyone inside, I'd like to see them. I want the crystal

34

bridge too, but you can put the far end of it in the next village instead of by the Tsar's palace."

His orders were carried out to the letter. His house came back and in it he found Aspid and the Tsarevna. They both slipped out as quickly as they could and went back to her father's palace.

When Aspid realized that the Tsarevna had lost the ring, he was so furious that he turned into a viper. He could never forgive her and so he stayed like that till the end of his days. All he could do was hiss at the Tsarevna and scold her. Her old father couldn't help remembering Semyon.

"He may only have been a peasant," he would say, "but at least he never turned into a snake."

Semyon and his mother were soon back in their old house, together with their cat and dog.

Now Semyon rides every day to the next village. It doesn't take long in a self-propelled carriage. They say he's asked for the hand of an orphan, a young girl who's even more beautiful than the Tsarevna.

Soon they'll be married and have children. And that will be the beginning of another story.

No-Arms

Once upon a time there was an old peasant who lived with his wife and two children. He came to the end of his life and he died. After that his wife prepared herself to die—soon it would be her turn. She called her children to her, her son and her daughter. Her daughter was the elder.

She said to her son:

"Obey your sister in everything, as you have obeyed me. Now she will be a mother to you."

She gave a last sigh—she was sorry to part with her children for ever—and she died.

After their parents' death the children began to live as their mother had told them. The brother obeyed his sister, and she looked after him and loved him.

And so they lived on without their parents, perhaps many years, perhaps few. One day the sister said to her brother:

"It's hard for me to keep house alone, and it's time you were married. Marry, then there'll be a mistress in the house."

The brother didn't want to marry.

"You're the mistress," he said. "Why do we need another?"

"I'll help her," said his sister. "The work will be easy with two of us."

The brother didn't want to marry, but he didn't dare disobey. He thought of her as his mother.

He married and began to live happily with his wife. He loved and respected his sister as before, obeying her in everything.

At first his wife didn't mind her sister-in-law. She thought she was very kind.

Later she grew jealous. She wanted to rule the house herself.

One day the young master went off to plough, or to market, or maybe into the forest. He came back to find trouble. His wife began complaining about her sister-in-law: she didn't know how to do anything properly, she was always in a bad temper, she'd just broken a new pot. . . .

The husband said nothing. He thought: "I leave home—at once there's trouble. That's bad."

But a man has to be away from home sometimes.

Once more the husband left home; once more he found trouble when he came back.

"It's your affair, but that sister of yours'll make beggars of us all. Just look in the barn! Our cow Zhdanka died yesterday. Your bitch of a sister fed her something and now the cow's dead."

What his wife didn't say was that she'd fed the cow poisonous grasses herself, just to be rid of her husband's sister.

The brother said to his sister:

"So you've poisoned the cow, sister. Well, we'll have to save a lot of money to buy another."

She was innocent but she didn't say anything—she didn't want her brother to think ill of his wife.

"I've made a mistake, brother," she answered. "It won't happen again."

"Well then," said her brother, "give me your blessing. I

must go to the forest and earn some money for the house. Look after everything, make sure nothing goes wrong. When my wife gives birth, help look after the child."

He went to the forest and was away from home a long time. His wife gave birth to a son; his sister looked after the child and loved him. He wasn't to live long though: one day his mother lay on him in her sleep and he died.

Just then the brother came back from the forest. At home —trouble. His wife howls and screams:

"It's that sister of yours, the snake in the grass; she's smothered our little son, she'll be the death of me next."

The brother heard his wife's words and was angry. He called his sister:

"I thought you were to be a mother to me. I've grudged you nothing, neither bread nor clothes, and I've always obeyed you. And now you've taken away my only son. He'd have been a hope and comfort to me when I'm old. He'd have fed you too, when you can't work any longer. And you've killed him.

"You will not live to see sunrise," he added.

His sister wanted to say something in answer, but her brother wouldn't listen to her in his grief and fury; he looked at her as though she were a stranger, as though he'd never seen her before.

He woke her before dawn.

"Get ready," he said, "we must be off."

"But, brother, it's early, it's not even light yet."

He didn't listen.

"Get ready, and put on your best dress."

"But, brother, it's not a holiday today."

Her brother was already harnessing the horses. They drove to the forest. It was still early, scarcely light.

In the forest was a tree-stump. He told her to kneel down and place her head on it.

38

The sister laid her arms on the stump, and her head on her arms.

"Forgive me, brother," she said, and she wanted to say how she hadn't done anything; maybe he'd listen to her now.

But he'd already lifted the axe high over his head. He had no time to listen.

Just then a bird called out in a gay, ringing voice. The sister lifted her head to listen, leaving her arms on the stump.

With the blow of his axe, her brother chopped off both her arms to the elbow. He could have forgiven no one the death of his son, not even his own mother.

"Quick!" he said. "Be off with you! Go where your eyes look! I'd wanted to cut off your head. It must be fate that you live."

He looked at his sister and wept. "Why is it," he thought, "that happiness is just happiness, while one sorrow always becomes two? Now I have no son, and no sister."

He rode away; his sister remained alone in the forest. She got up and set off, with no arms, where her eyes looked. The paths were all overgrown and she had no idea where they led. Soon there weren't even overgrown paths. She was lost, weak with hunger, her dress torn to rags.

Days passed; nights passed; she still followed her eyes. She wasn't used to having no arms and she missed her brother. She walked on, crying:

> Winds, winds, unruly winds,
> Take my tears to my mother,
> Take them to my father.
> But I have no mother, I have no father.
> Sun, sun, high in the sky,
> Give warmth to me, unhappy me.

The world before her was all clouded in tears, and she couldn't wipe them away. She walked on, not seeing how the wind combed her hair and the sun brightened her cheeks, making her again grow fair and lovely. It must be true what they say—that good people are made beautiful by sorrow, while evil people are disfigured even by beauty.

When her tears dried, there was an orchard, the forest had gone. There were apples ripening on the trees—big, juicy ones. Some of them grew quite low—you could reach them with your mouth. She ate one apple and had a bite of a second, but that was all: she was eating what belonged to a stranger for the first time—forced to by hunger.

Then the watchman came up and started shouting:

"You witch! What's brought you here, grabbing other people's apples in your mouth? I've watched this orchard thirty years and not one apple's been stolen. And now you come along and start munching. You'll catch it, thief with no arms!"

The watchman cursed her roundly and took her to his master.

Just then the master's young son was sitting in the cottage. He saw a young girl; she was thin and wretched, quite plain at first glance, but the kindness in her eyes made her more beautiful than any beauty could, more beautiful than anyone. He wondered at this strange girl, his heart beating with joy.

"Let her go!" he shouted to the watchman. He went up to her and saw she had no arms. He loved her still more—someone you love, you love—crippled or not.

But then he became worried: what would his father say?

He went to his father, bowed, and said:

"Father, I have news to tell you; of joy, not of sorrow.

"Our watchman's caught a girl in the orchard and there's no one I love more in the world. Don't break my heart, Father. Allow me to marry her."

His father went out of the house, looked at the girl with no arms, and said:

"What's the matter with you, son? There are plenty of girls who're prettier than she is—and richer. Look at her—an armless cripple! You'll end up carrying her begging bowl for her."

The son replied:

"There may be prettier girls in the world, but none I love more. And as for the begging bowl, well, Father, if that's our fate, so be it."

His father thought for a moment.

"Make up your own mind, son! I have power in my house and power in my orchard, but I have no power in your heart. A heart's not an apple."

A joyful wedding was held, and the young ones began to live together. They lived together peacefully and happily— but not for long.

War began; the husband of the girl with no arms was called to the army. When he was ready to go, he spoke to his father:

"Be kind to my wife, Father. It won't be long till she gives birth. Write to me then. Tell me whether to give thanks for a son or a daughter."

"God be with you, son! Take care! Don't lay down your life for nothing. You'll miss your wife, but don't worry yourself about her; she'll be like my own daughter to me."

And the young man set off to the war. Soon his wife with no arms bore him a son. The mother looked at her child; the grandfather looked; they saw—the boy's hands were of gold, the moon shone bright on his forehead, and where his heart was, there was the sun. Yes, that's how all children are to a mother or to a grandfather.

The grandfather set off to take his apples to market. The mother with no arms called the old watchman and told him to write a letter to her husband. Long ago the old man had served in the army and had learnt to write. First, she told him to send greetings—from herself and from her father-in-law—and then to say how she'd given birth to a fine son, and to say everything about him, why it was that everyone who looked at him was glad.

The old man wrote out the letter, hid it inside his shirt, and set off.

He walked through forests, through fields. Night fell. Not far away was a hut. He asked to stay the night there.

The owners took him in and gave him supper. The wife put out some bedding for him. The husband lay down and fell asleep, but the wife began to ask the old man questions: who were his people; where had he come from and where was he going; and how had he lived to be old—through good times or bad times, in plenty or in hunger. The old man told how he'd lived before and what his business was now.

"Now," he said, "I'm taking good news to the young master: his wife has borne him a son. And his wife has no arms, but her face is kind, and no one in the world can have a kinder heart."

The woman looked surprised.

"Hasn't she any arms at all?"

"No," said the old man, "I've heard her own brother chopped them off—I suppose it was just out of hate."

The woman looked even more surprised.

"My God! What villains there are in the world! But where've you put your news? Take care you don't lose it!"

"Here it is," said the old man, "in a paper inside my shirt."

"Why don't you go and steam yourself a bit in the bathhouse?" said the woman. "You must be worn out by now and you'll have sweated a good bit on the road. I'll stoke it up right away!"

The old man was glad. "There's never any harm in a bath," he thought.

The woman stoked up the bath-house. The old man took

off his clothes and went to steam out his bones. But it wasn't out of respect or kindness of heart that the woman prepared the bath for the traveller: her husband was No-Arms' brother, he'd taken her from here to the forest, but he hadn't cut off her head.

She found the letter inside the old man's shirt and read it through; then she threw it into the stove, wrote out another one, and put it back where the first one had been. In this letter was written that the wife had borne her husband not a son, but something like a piglet in front, like a dog from behind, and with a back like a hedgehog, and as for what was to be done with it—let her husband decide.

Morning came. The old man went on his way.

Time passed. There was the same old man, coming back by the same road. The woman saw him and called him into the hut.

The old man stayed the night. The woman asked him what he was taking home and what the young master had said to him.

"I didn't see the master: he was fighting. After the battle was over, I received a letter from him. In it he has stated his will."

"What is his will?" asked the woman.

"I don't know," said the old man. "It isn't for me to read his letter."

The old man got ready to lie down to sleep: it was already dark.

The woman said to him:

"Let me darn your shirt, Grandad. It's full of holes."

The old man was already asleep. She took his shirt and looked inside. There was the letter. She unsewed it and began to read. It was from the husband to his wife with no arms: in it he told her to pity and take care of the child, and as for it being misshapen, he would love and cherish it none the less;

43

he also begged his father to look after the child and care for him.

"No," whispered the woman, "your father will not look after the child."

And she wrote another letter. It was from the husband to his father: in it he asked his father to turn his wife out of the house together with her son: he didn't want to know any more of her; why should he live with a wife with no arms? she was no mate for a warrior; and if he lived through the war, he'd marry again.

She darned the shirt and sewed her own letter into the lining.

Next morning the old man went on his way.

He came to his master, No-Arms' father-in-law, and gave him the letter.

The father-in-law read the letter and called No-Arms.

"Good day, mistress!"

"Good day, Father! But what kind of mistress am I here? I'm the youngest in the house."

The old father-in-law thought for a moment.

"Yes," he said, "and I'm no master. When the watchman brought you in, I wanted to drive you away, but you stayed. And now I want you to live all your life in my house, but you must leave for ever."

And he told her what was in the letter.

"He tells me to drive you out of the house. His heart must have changed to you."

In the morning No-Arms took her baby son in the fold of her skirt, caught the edge of the hem in her teeth, and left. She went where everyone goes who has nowhere to go to—where her eyes looked.

And the old father-in-law was left alone in the house. He began to miss his grandson and his daughter-in-law with no arms.

He called the old watchman from the orchard and told him to search for No-Arms and her son, and to bring them back home. The watchman set off through the woods and fields and wandered there a long time, calling for No-Arms. But the world's a big place—how could he hope to find them? He returned empty-handed.

The old father-in-law began to grieve and pine; one day he lay down to sleep and didn't wake up—he died of sorrow.

No-Arms had left the house and followed her eyes. She became thirsty as she walked through the open fields. Then she came to the forest. In the forest was an old grandfather-oak, and not far from the oak a well. She bent down over the well, but the water was too deep, she couldn't drink. She bent down lower. There it was, water. "At least I can wet my lips," she thought.

Her lips touched the water, she unclenched her teeth, and down fell her child, out of her skirt and into the well. His mother stretched after him, remembered about her arms, and wept. "Alas," she thought, "why was I born? I'm strong enough to bear grief and injury. I was strong enough to bear the loss of my arms. I was strong enough to give birth to a child and yet now I'm too weak to save him."

Through the water she could still see her son lying at the bottom of the well. And then she saw her arms had grown—she stretched them out to her child and seized him. And after she'd caught him up from the water, after she'd saved him—again she had no arms.

No-Arms set off once more with the son she had saved. As it got dark she came to a village. She asked to stay the night there. In the morning she was ready to go further, but the people in that village were kind: they took in the mother with no arms, so she could live there and bring up her child among them.

No-Arms' son grew up among kind people, but the war where his father was fighting had still not finished. Wars went on a long time in those days.

Time went by—No-Arms' son was called to the war too. His mother fitted him out so he should have everything he needed; the whole village helped. They bought him clothing and victuals. They bought him a horse—let him ride to the war! His mother bade farewell to her only son.

"Go," she said, "and come back alive. Your father's fighting there. Now it's your turn, my son. If the enemy invades, we shall all die; if you drive him out, we need never be parted again."

Her son rode off to the war. His mother was left alone, yearning for him. She thought of him all day and dreamed of him all night. Sometimes she saw him lying dead in a field, crows pecking his eyes.

Her heart couldn't bear it—she dressed herself as a soldier and set off to the war.

When she arrived, some soldiers saw her. They thought she was a man and said:

"You should have stayed at home by the stove, friend! What can a cripple do in a war? You're a brave fellow, but this is no place for you."

But No-Arms knew where her place was. She began to care for the sick and the dying: often someone would be about to die, she'd speak to him—and he'd live; or a soldier would lose heart, she'd go before him against the enemy, and once more he would lift up his sword.

Once No-Arms caught sight of her son. He was out on the battle-field and the enemy were falling dead around him. He was hard pressed. Everyone who'd fought by his side had fallen. He was alone. But in place of the enemies he killed, came more, and there was no end to them.

His mother watched—would her son hold out or not? His

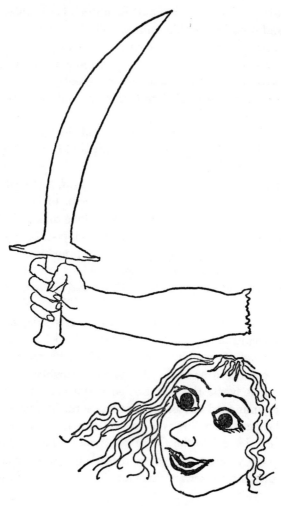

arm was powerful, but all power can be overpowered. And then a whole host fell on him. She couldn't even see her son. She didn't know if he was alive or dead.

From a distance the commander himself was watching the battle. He said to his aide:

47

"Find out what warrior of ours is fighting there, whose son he is, and send help to him immediately!"

But when would this help come? In time or too late? No-Arms saw her son rise from the ground and a black host bear down on him. It was her time. She cried out:

"Stand firm, my son! Stand firm, my only son!"—and threw herself to his side.

She had forgotten she had no arms—all she knew was her heart beating in fury against the enemy and in love for her son—and then she felt them again, and the strength in them, as though her brother had never cut them off. She snatched up the sword of a dead warrior and began to hew at the enemies around her son. She fought for a long time, shielding him; she was tiring; her son was soaked in blood, barely able to stand. Then help came from the commander. Fresh soldiers cut down those of the enemy who were left; those who had fallen at the hands of No-Arms and her son already lay dead.

No-Arms' son had fought by his mother's side, but he hadn't recognized her: he hadn't had time to look at her, and even if he had, he wouldn't have known her—his mother had no arms but the arms of this warrior were mighty.

After that battle the war was soon finished. The commander summoned all the bravest warriors: he asked each where he came from and who was his father, and gave each his reward. He called the son of No-Arms and asked him:

"Who are your people, young man? Who are your father and mother? I must reward them too, for having raised such a son."

No-Arms' son hung his head.

"I have no father," he said, "and I cannot remember who he was. I grew up alone with my mother. The earth was our bed and the sky our covering. Good people took the place of my father."

"The people are a father to all fathers," said the commander. "I am less than they, and cannot reward them. But your mother must be rewarded—she has raised a brave son. Let her come before me and take her reward in her hands."

"But she has no hands, she has no arms at all," said her son.

The commander looked sadly and penetratingly at the young warrior.

"Go," he said, "and bring your mother before me."

No-Arms' son went back to the village. There they told him how his mother had gone to the war. She'd gone to care for the sick and the dying.

He went back and told the commander. The commander ordered everyone who'd cared for the wounded to be brought before him. He began to reward them for their good work. And when a woman with no arms came before him, he looked her full in the face and knew her as his wife, and No-Arms saw that this general was her husband. No-Arms wanted to embrace him—she had been separated from him for a whole age—but she remembered she had no arms. They had withered again after she had saved her son. But No-Arms couldn't bear it. She stretched towards her husband. She had always loved him and never forgotten. And at that moment, as though from her heart, her arms grew, as strong as they had ever been, and with them she embraced her husband. After that her arms stayed for ever.

Then the father called his son and said to him:

"Greetings, my son! I am your father, and you did not know me, nor I you. Evil people parted us, but there is a power more powerful than evil."

The son looked at his father and was glad. Then he looked at his mother and saw she had hands and arms. He remembered that last battle and the warrior who had shielded him with his sword. He fell on his knees before her and kissed her hands that had saved him.

49

Soon, when times were peaceful, the commander set off to the house where he had once lived with his father, where he had first met No-Arms and loved her. He took with him his wife and his son and rode off to live in peace. On the way they stopped at the hut of No-Arms' brother.

The brother's wife saw who had come—No-Arms herself and all her family, all in good health, all famous—collapsed at their feet in terror, and at once told them all she had done to destroy No-Arms and her child.

"Maybe they will forgive me," she thought, "it was a long time ago."

No-Arms listened to her, and in answer told of her own fate, all she had suffered.

No-Arms' brother bowed to his sister, and said:

"Thank you for what you have told, but evil must not be left to bear seed. Forgive me, sister."

That night, unseen by his guests, he took from the stables a young mare that wasn't yet broken in, twisted the reins, tied his wife to the tail and himself to his wife, cried out—and the horse was off, dragging husband and wife through the open fields, beating them to death against the ground.

In the morning, No-Arms and her husband and son waited for their hosts, but only a mare came, alone, with no rider, from out of the open fields.

The guests rode off to live long years at home. Unhappiness lives in the world, but by chance; happiness must live for ever.

The Angry Tsaritsa

Once, many years ago, there lived an angry Tsaritsa. She was always angry with everything and everyone and there was nothing anyone could do about it.

One day she went for a walk in the garden. There was a soldier on sentry-duty who'd never seen her before. The Tsaritsa was very pretty and the soldier grinned at her. He was new at Court and he didn't know that one must neither grin, frown, nor even look respectfully at the Tsaritsa. She flew off the handle whatever one did.

The Tsaritsa scowled at him:

"Why are you smirking like that?" she shouted.

The poor soldier didn't know what to say. He just smirked even more. The Tsaritsa was speechless with rage. When she recovered, she called one of her ministers.

"Have this soldier given twelve stripes every morning!" she ordered.

Every day after that the soldier was given twelve stripes as soon as he got up in the morning.

It went on like this every day for a year. It was the same

even on holidays. The poor man was getting worn out. Soon there wouldn't be anything left of him to beat. As for the Tsaritsa, she'd forgotten about him long ago. She didn't mind whether or not he was beaten to death.

The soldier began asking other people for advice. He could see he had to do something soon or it would be the end of him. First he asked all the clever people. They all said:

"Be patient. She's an angry Tsaritsa. There's nothing anyone can do about it."

"It's all right for some people," thought the soldier and went along to ask the fool what he thought.

The fool had lived with the soldiers for a long time. They let him have scraps of food from the kitchen and gave him their old clothes to wear out.

The soldier began to explain his troubles but the fool stopped him. He knew all about it already.

"Anyway, I don't know why I'm telling you," said the soldier. "You're just a fool. You won't be able to help."

"The more fool you to ask advice from a fool," said the fool. "Still, you've got nothing to lose. Just give me a kopeck."

The soldier gave him a kopeck and they went together to the outskirts of town. They walked a very long way indeed. They went past all the palaces and came to the huts where the peasants lived.

The soldier began to get worried. He thought the fool was just making fun of him.

Then they went into one of the huts. It belonged to an old cobbler.

This cobbler had a wife who looked just like the Tsaritsa. She could have been her twin sister. He used to show her to people for one kopeck and then spend the money on drink. Soldiers and cripples were allowed in free.

The fool paid his kopeck and the soldier went in free. They

52

found a woman asleep on a bed. She was the very image of the Tsaritsa. The soldier jumped to attention.

"Now if she was the Tsaritsa, she wouldn't beat you every morning," said the fool.

"You're right," said the soldier. "She'd have made a fine Tsaritsa. What a pity she's only a cobbler's wife."

"She will make a fine Tsaritsa," said the fool and began to laugh.

"What do you mean?" asked the soldier.

The fool was splitting his sides by then. The soldier was afraid he'd wake the cobbler's wife. He led him out of the room.

On their way back the fool asked:

"Where are you doing sentry-duty tonight?"

"In the palace, by the Tsaritsa's chamber."

"Fine! Then I'll bring you the cobbler's wife tonight."

"You fool!" said the soldier. "What about the cobbler?"

"He won't notice. He works like a horse, drinks like a fish and sleeps all night like a log. It would take an earthquake to wake him up."

"Anyway, what do you want me to do with the cobbler's wife?"

"Who's the fool now?" said the fool. He went on to explain: "Take the Tsaritsa when she's fast asleep, hand her over to me, and I'll give you the cobbler's wife. You lay the cobbler's wife in the Tsaritsa's chamber and I'll take the Tsaritsa back to the cobbler's."

The soldier thought for a moment:

"But what if the Tsaritsa wakes up? She'll have us both executed before you can say Jack Robinson."

"She won't wake up," said the fool. "She screams and rages all day and by evening she's flat out. You can hear her snoring all over the palace. Anyway, I'm a fool. I can't be punished."

53

"Well," agreed the soldier, "you may be a fool but your head's certainly screwed on all right. Bring me the cobbler's wife tonight."

That night the cobbler's wife was laid in the Tsaritsa's chamber and the Tsaritsa was taken all the way to the cobbler's. Neither of them woke up.

Next morning the cobbler woke up and gave his wife a dig in the ribs. He had a headache and he wanted something to drink. He wanted his wife to fetch him his pipe and some water and say something to make things better.

The Tsaritsa woke up and opened her eyes. She thought she was dreaming and went back to sleep again.

The cobbler gave her another dig in the ribs.

"Come on, woman, it's time you were up. What's the matter with you today?"

The Tsaritsa half-opened her eyes:

"Who are you? What are you doing here?"

"And who do you think you are all of a sudden?"

The Tsaritsa was furious:

"You rascal! You wicked scoundrel! I'll teach you how to speak to the Tsaritsa."

The cobbler jumped straight out of bed.

"Oh! So you're the Tsaritsa, are you?"

He seized a leather belt and gave her a good whipping.

"Take that, you wretch! A fine Tsaritsa you'd make! Take that! And that! I'll teach you to lie in bed all morning."

"Whip the scoundrel to death!" screamed the Tsaritsa.

No one took any notice. The Tsaritsa thought she must have died. Now she was in hell and being tormented by devils.

She turned over and tried to go to sleep again. Maybe it was all just a nightmare. Soon she'd wake up again in her own palace and everything would be the same as it always had been.

The devil laid down his strap and punched her again in the ribs.

"Get yourself out of bed, woman!"

"Leave me alone. I'm the Tsaritsa."

"Still playing at that, are we?" said the cobbler and started whipping her again. "Come on, woman! I've told you three

times to get up now. Boil the potatoes, heat up the samovar, tidy the room and get my socks darned. Quick!"

By now the Tsaritsa was growing timid. She was scared of this devil who beat her and whipped her. It hurt terribly. It hurt all the more for being the first time in her life she'd ever known pain. She started trying to do the housework. She'd never done anything before except be an angry Tsaritsa and she found it very difficult. She kept knocking things over and spilling everything on the floor.

The cobbler saw what a mess she was making and started beating her again. This time she didn't say a word about being a Tsaritsa. She just went on with her work.

Somehow or other she got lunch together, but everything was too salty, the vegetables were half raw and there were bits of grit in the soup.

The cobbler took one mouthful and spat it out.

"Maybe you really are a Tsaritsa. Not even a pig would eat this."

He got out his whip and gave her another thrashing.

After that the Tsaritsa was terrified. She just sat there and trembled.

The cobbler lay down for a rest.

"I'm going to doze off for a while. You take a comb and give my head a good scratch."

The Tsaritsa began scratching. There wasn't much else she could do.

The next day the cobbler told her to do the washing. She scrubbed and scrubbed. She scrubbed all the skin off her hands and the clothes were still dirty.

It went on like this for three days. The Tsaritsa had never known anything like it.

Meanwhile the cobbler's wife had woken up in the Tsaritsa's chamber. She was lying between silk sheets on a mattress of soft down. The walls and ceilings were beautifully painted. There were lots of mirrors and fine carpets. The whole room was full of flowers.

The cobbler's wife had never seen anything like it. She thought she must be in heaven.

The cook and the kitchen-maids treated her with great respect. They gave her all the sugar she asked for. They all seemed to think she was the Tsaritsa. Soon she even began to think so herself.

"Who knows?" she said. "Maybe I really am a Tsaritsa.

Why shouldn't I be Tsaritsa for a while? It won't do my husband any harm. He'll just have to look after himself. I can always be a cobbler's wife again later."

She was Tsaritsa for three whole days. Wherever she went, she was followed by a minister who carried out all her commands. Whenever someone came to her with a petition, she just said:

"Ask the man behind. He knows."

On the afternoon of the second day the cobbler's wife was walking round the gardens munching sunflower seeds. Her minister carried great handfuls of them for her. She just had to stretch out her hand and he would pour some out. It was a great honour for him.

Our soldier was on duty beside a wooden sentry-box. The Tsaritsa and her minister were walking towards him.

He was watching the Tsaritsa out of the corner of his eye. He tried so hard to look serious that in the end he just smirked.

"Why are you grinning like that?" asked the cobbler's wife. "Is it just that you're glad to see me?"

"That's right, Mother. I'm glad to see you."

"Why? I've never done anything for you. There must be something you want."

"Tell them to stop beating me, Mother. They whip me every day as soon as I get up. It's over a year since they started. They've whipped nearly all the flesh off my bones."

"Why do they beat you?"

"Because I smirked, Mother."

"All right then. Speak to the man behind. He'll tell them to stop beating you."

"No," said the soldier. "I don't want to speak to the man behind. You're in front. You give the order yourself."

"All right, I'll write out an order and I'll sign it myself. Anything to be left in peace."

57

"And say that the others shouldn't be beaten either."

"Why, do many people get beaten here?"

"Yes, Mother, there's hardly anyone who doesn't. Everyone at Court's been beaten black and blue, but they still don't complain."

"What, are they all idiots?"

"I don't know, Mother."

That day the cobbler's wife decreed that no one in all her kingdom should ever be beaten and that no one should even dare touch another man with a stick.

She also ordered that all her soldiers were to be given twenty-five roubles and half a barrel of beer. There was to be a three-day holiday for the whole country.

On the third day of her reign the cobbler's wife began to miss her husband.

"I'll just go and see what he's up to. He's probably begun to miss me by now."

The cobbler's wife left the palace and walked back to her old home. Her minister followed behind.

Just as she caught sight of the house, the cobbler came out of the door. He was with another woman. She was just as beautiful as the cobbler's wife herself. The cobbler's wife could hardly believe her eyes.

She grabbed her husband by the collar and began shaking him about. His cap flew way down the street.

The cobbler didn't know what had hit him. He looked first at one woman, then at the other. They were as like as two peas.

He only knew which was his wife when she started pummelling him on the back. She seized him by the arm and dragged him into the house. She'd forgotten about her new kingdom by then.

The Tsaritsa glared furiously at her minister and set off towards the palace.

When she got back, she learnt about the new decree. No one in all her kingdom was ever to be beaten, birched, whipped or flogged. This decree had been made in her own name.

The Tsaritsa was furious. She went straight to her rooms and called out the first names that came to her head. She wanted someone to beat.

The cook came in first. The Tsaritsa was about to start beating her when she caught sight of the blisters and sores on her own hand. She paused for a moment and let it fall to her side.

She'd remembered what it had been like at the cobbler's. She thought she'd better leave the decree as it was. Who knows? One day she might be turned into a cobbler's wife again.

The soldier and the fool were very pleased with themselves. And neither of them were ever afraid of Tsars or Tsaritsas for the rest of their lives.

Phoenist the Bright Falcon

※※※※※※❖❖❖※※※※※※

Once upon a time there was a farmer who lived in a village with his wife and three daughters. As the daughters grew up, so the parents grew older, and one fine day the old mother died. Now the farmer had to bring up his three daughters by himself. They were all of them beautiful, and each as beautiful as the others, but their tempers were different.

The old farmer was well off and he didn't want his daughters to have to work too hard. He was going to find some lonely old widow to keep house, but Mary, his youngest daughter, said:

"Father, there's no need to look for anyone. I can keep house by myself."

Mary was very kind. The older daughters didn't say a word.

And so Mary began to keep house for them all. She knew everything; if there was anything she didn't know, she soon learnt it. Her father watched; he was very glad his daughter was so clever, good-tempered and hard-working. She was beautiful too, and all the more beautiful for her kindness. Her sisters were also beautiful, but they never thought they were beautiful enough, and they were always trying to make themselves even more beautiful by putting on different powders and rouges and trying on new dresses. The two older sisters would sit there all day dressing themselves up and in the evening they looked just the same as they always had done. They'd realize they'd wasted a whole day and used up all their make-up without becoming any more beautiful, and they'd sit there, getting crosser and crosser. Mary would be tired out by evening, but she'd know that she'd fed the animals and cleaned the house, cooked the supper and baked the bread, and that her father would be pleased with her. She'd look at her sisters with kind eyes and not say a word. That made her sisters even more cross. They thought that Mary was more beautiful now than she'd been in the morning and they couldn't understand why.

One day the father had to go to market. He asked his daughters:

"Well, children, what shall I buy you? What do you need to make you happy?"

The eldest daughter said:

"Buy me a shawl, Father, one with big flowers embroidered on it in gold."

"You can buy me a shawl too, Father," said the middle daughter, "one with big flowers embroidered on it in gold, and with red in the centre of each flower. And buy me some boots as well, with soft calves and with high heels that bang on the ground."

The eldest daughter was very greedy and she was furious with her sister. She said to her father:

"And get the same for me, Father. Get me some boots with soft calves and heels that bang on the ground. And buy me a beautiful ring as well—after all, I'm your only eldest daughter."

The father promised to buy all the presents his two older daughters had asked for. Then he asked his youngest daughter:

"Mary, why are you so quiet there?"

"I don't want anything, Father. I never leave the house. I don't need any fine clothes."

"Don't talk like that, Mary. How can I leave you out? I must get you a little fairing."

"I don't need a fairing," said the youngest daughter, "but, Father, if it's not too expensive, buy me a feather of Phoenist the bright falcon."

The father rode off to market. He bought all the presents his older daughters had asked for, but there was nowhere he could find a feather of Phoenist the bright falcon.

"No," the merchants would say, "we haven't got anything like that, there's no demand."

The father didn't want to disappoint his clever, hard-working youngest daughter, but what could he do? He went back home without buying a feather of Phoenist the bright falcon.

Mary didn't mind.

"Never mind, Father," she said. "You'll be able to get it next time."

Some time later the father had to go to market again. He asked his daughters what presents they wanted: he was very kind.

The eldest daughter said:

"Last time, Father, you brought me some boots. Now you must get the blacksmith to heel them with silver horse-shoes."

The middle daughter listened to her sister and said:

"And do the same for me, Father. Else the heels just bang on the ground. I want them to ring. And so I don't lose the nails from the horse-shoes, buy me a little silver hammer so I can hammer them in."

"And what do you want, Mary?"

"Have a look round, Father. See if you can find a feather of Phoenist the bright falcon."

The old man rode off to market. He soon finished his own business and bought his two older daughters their presents. Then he began to look for Mary's feather. He searched till it was dark but he couldn't find one anywhere. Again he came back without a present for his youngest daughter. He felt sorry for Mary, but she just smiled at him. She was happy simply to see him again.

Time passed. Once more the father had to go to market.

"Well, daughters, what presents shall I buy you?"

The eldest daughter thought and thought and couldn't think what she wanted.

"Father, buy me something beautiful."

The middle daughter said:

"Father, buy me something beautiful too, and then buy me something even more beautiful."

"What about you, Mary?"

"I just want a feather of Phoenist the bright falcon."

The old man rode off to market. He finished his own business and bought his older daughters their presents, but he couldn't get anything for Mary. There wasn't anyone in the market who sold feathers.

On his way home the father saw an old, old man walking along the road. He'd never seen anyone so old in all his life.

"Good day, Grandfather."

"Good day, fellow. What are you so sad about?"

"How can I help it? My daughter keeps asking me to buy a feather of Phoenist the bright falcon. I've searched and searched, but I can't find one anywhere. And it's for my youngest daughter, the one I love most of all."

The old man thought for a moment and said:

"Well, so be it!"

He untied the bag he carried over his shoulder and took out a little box.

"Keep the box somewhere safe," he said. "There's a feather of Phoenist the bright falcon inside. Now listen: I have a son and I love him as much as you love your daughter. It's time he was married, but he doesn't want to and I can't force him. And he keeps saying: if anyone asks for this feather, give it to him. The girl who wants it will be my sweetheart."

The old, old man said all this—and suddenly he wasn't there any more. He'd vanished. Perhaps he'd never been there at all.

Mary's father stood there alone, holding the feather in his hands. He looked at it—it was grey and ordinary. But he hadn't been able to buy it anywhere.

The father remembered the old man's words and thought: "Well, I suppose that will be her fate: she'll marry someone she's never known and never seen."

He came home, gave the older daughters their presents, and gave Mary the little box with the grey feather.

The older sisters put on their new dresses and began to laugh at Mary.

"Go on then! Stick your feather in your hair and go and look at yourself in the mirror."

Mary didn't say a word, but when everyone in the cottage had gone to sleep, she laid the plain, grey feather in front of her on the table and wondered at it. Then she picked it up in her hands and held it against her breast. She began to stroke it, but it fell on the floor.

At once there was a knock at the window. The window opened and in flew Phoenist the bright falcon. He touched the floor and turned into a handsome young prince. Mary closed the window and she and her prince began to talk to each other. When it was nearly morning, she opened the window. The prince bent down to the floor, turned himself into a bright falcon, left one plain grey feather behind, and flew off into the blue sky.

Three nights Mary talked with her falcon. All day he flew about the sky, over fields and forests, above mountains and oceans; in the evening he flew to his Mary and became a handsome prince.

The fourth night the older sisters heard Mary talking, and they heard the prince's voice too, and they asked her next morning:

"Well, sister, who is it you talk to at nights?"

"I talk to myself," answered Mary. "I have no friends, I work all day and I haven't got time to talk; at nights I talk a bit with myself."

The older sisters didn't believe her.

They told their father:

"Father, our Mary's got herself a young man. They see each other every night. We've heard them talking."

"You oughtn't to listen," said their father. "Why shouldn't she have a young man? There's nothing wrong in that. She's beautiful and she's the right age. It will be your turn next."

"But it's my turn now," said the eldest daughter. "I should be the first to marry."

"True enough," agreed the father. "But life's like that. One girl stays an old maid to the end of her days, and another gets courted by everyone."

As he was saying this, the father thought to himself: "Perhaps what the old man said has come true. I don't mind if it has, but I'd like to have a look at her young man."

The two older daughters had their own ideas. As soon as it was getting dark they went into Mary's room, stuck knives all round the frame of the window and filled in the spaces with splinters of wood and bits of broken glass. Mary was cleaning out the cowshed then and she didn't see anything.

65

When it was quite dark, Phoenist the bright falcon came to Mary's window. He flew straight into a wall of knives and splinters and slivers of jagged glass. He struggled and struggled and tore open all his chest. Mary was worn out after the day's work and she'd gone to sleep while she was waiting for him. She didn't hear him struggling in the window.

Phoenist cried out in a loud voice:

"Goodbye, my love! If you need me, you will find me, wherever I am. But on your way you will wear out three pairs of iron shoes, you will wear down three iron staffs against the wayside grass, and you will swallow three stone loaves."

Mary heard Phoenist's words through her sleep, but she wasn't able to wake up. When she woke up in the morning, she felt sad. She looked at the window and saw Phoenist's blood drying in the sun. She began to weep. She opened the window and buried her face in Phoenist's blood. Her tears washed the blood away and her own face became even more beautiful. It was as though she'd just bathed it.

Mary went to her father and said to him:

"Don't be angry with me, Father. I must set off on a journey. If I stay alive, we'll meet again; if I die, that's how it was fated."

Her father didn't want his dearest, youngest daughter to set off heaven knows where. But what could he do? He couldn't make her stay at home. He knew that a girl's loving heart is more powerful than a father's will. He blessed his favourite daughter and told her she could go.

The blacksmith made Mary three pairs of iron shoes and three iron staffs and she took three stone loaves. Then she curtsied to her father and sisters, visited her mother's grave, and set off to find Phoenist the bright falcon.

She walked more than a day, more than two days, more than three days—no one knows how many. She walked over open fields and through dark forests. She crossed high

mountains. Birds sang to her in the fields; the dark forests treated her kindly; as she walked through the high mountains she could see the whole world. She walked on and on. She wore out one pair of iron shoes. She wore down one iron staff against the wayside grass. She ate one stone loaf. Still she hadn't finished her journey, still there was no sign of Phoenist the bright falcon.

She sighed, sat down on the ground, and was just putting on her second pair of iron shoes when she saw a cottage on the edge of the forest. By now it was almost night. Mary decided to go and ask if anyone there had seen Phoenist the bright falcon.

She knocked on the door. She could see an old woman inside. She wondered if she was kind or wicked. The old woman opened the door. Before her she saw a beautiful young girl.

"Grandmother, let me stay the night here."

"Come in, love, you're welcome. Is it far you're going?"

"I don't know, Grandmother. I'm looking for Phoenist the bright falcon. Grandmother, you haven't heard about him, have you?"

"What do you mean? Of course I have! I'm old, I've been living a long time, I've heard about everyone. You've got a long way to go, my dear."

In the morning the old woman woke Mary up and said to her:

"Wake up, love, you must go and see my middle sister. She's older than me and she knows more than I do. Maybe she'll tell you where your Phoenist lives. And so you don't forget me, take this silver distaff and golden spindle."

Mary took the gift, gazed at it in wonder and said to the old woman:

"Thank you, Grandmother. But tell me, which way should I go?"

"I'll give you a magic ball. Follow it wherever it rolls. When you need a rest, just sit down on the grass—it'll stop and wait for you."

Mary curtsied to the old woman and set off after the magic ball. She walked a long way—no one knows how far. The forests were dark and terrible, the fields were full of thistles instead of corn, the mountains were gaunt and rocky, and the birds didn't sing. The further Mary travelled, the faster she went. Then she had to change her shoes again. She'd worn out her second pair of iron shoes. She'd ground down her second iron staff. She'd eaten a second stone loaf.

Mary sat down. She looked round. It was nearly dark. Not far away, on the very edge of the forest, she could see a little cottage. There was a light burning in the window.

The magic ball rolled up to the cottage. Mary followed. She knocked at the window.

"Good people, let me come in."

A very old woman came out onto the porch. She was even older than the first one.

"Where are you going, young girl? Who is it you're looking for?"

"I'm looking for Phoenist the bright falcon. I found an old woman in the forest and stayed the night at her cottage. She'd heard about Phoenist, but she didn't know where I could find him. She said that maybe her older sister would know."

The old woman let Mary into the cottage. In the morning she woke her and said:

"You'll have to go a long way to find Phoenist. I know about him, but I've never seen him. You must go to our eldest sister. She'll have seen him. And so you don't forget me, take this as a gift. It'll be a help in need, and a keepsake in joy."

And the old woman gave her guest a silver saucer and a golden egg.

Mary said goodbye, curtsied to the old woman, and set off after the magic ball.

She walked on. The country around her became quite strange. There were no fields any more, just forest. And the further the ball rolled, the higher the trees grew. It became quite dark. You couldn't see the sun or the sky.

Mary walked on through the darkness. She wore out her last pair of iron shoes. She ground down her last iron staff. She ate the last crumb of her last stone loaf.

She looked round—she didn't know what to do. Then she saw her magic ball. It was lying under the window of a little cottage.

Mary knocked at the window.

"Kind people, shelter me from the dark night."

An old, old woman came out onto the porch, the eldest of all the three sisters.

"Come in, love," she said. "What a long, long way you've come! No one lives further on in the world—I'm the last one. Tomorrow you must go back again. But who are your people and where are you going?"

"I'm not from these parts, Grandmother," said Mary, "and I'm searching for Phoenist the bright falcon."

The old, old woman looked hard at Mary and said:

"So you're looking for Phoenist, are you? I know him. I've been living so long I've got to know everyone. I can remember everyone in the world."

She put Mary to bed. In the morning she woke her up and said to her:

"It's a long time since I've done anyone any good. I live alone in the forest. I remember everyone but no one remembers me. I can do you a good turn though—I can tell you where Phoenist the bright falcon lives. But it won't be easy

70

for you even if you do find him. He's married now and he lives with his wife. You'll have a hard time. Still you're strong and you've got a good heart. Where there's a will, there's a way."

"Thank you, Grandmother," said Mary, and she curtsied very low, right down to the ground.

"You can thank me afterwards. Now here's a present for you—take this golden needle and thimble: you hold the thimble, and the needle will sew by itself. Well, be off with you now. You'll find out what to do next as you go along."

The magic ball didn't roll any further. The old, old woman came out onto the porch and showed Mary which way to go.

Mary set off the way she'd come, barefoot. The earth was hard and unfriendly. She was afraid she'd never reach Phoenist.

Then she came to a rich house in a clearing. It had tall towers and an iron gate. There was a rich important-looking woman looking out of one of the windows. She seemed to be wondering what Mary was doing there.

Mary remembered that she hadn't got any shoes and that she'd eaten her last stone loaf.

She said to the woman:

"Good day to you! Do you need someone to work in your house for bread and clothing?"

"I do," said the important-looking woman. "But do you know how to make a fire, and fetch water, and cook dinner?"

"I lived with a father and no mother. I can do everything."

"And do you know how to spin and sew and embroider?"

Mary remembered the presents the old women had given her.

"Yes," she said.

"Go along to the kitchen then," said the important-looking woman.

And so Mary began working in a strange, rich house. She was honest and she was quick with her hands. There was nothing she couldn't do.

The mistress of the house could hardly believe her luck. She had never had a maid who was so hard-working, so kind and so quick-witted. The only thing she ate was plain bread. She washed it down with a kind of weak beer called kvass and never even asked for tea. The mistress began to boast to her daughter:

"Look what a good maid I've found: she's clever and she does what she's told and she's got such a kind face."

The mistress's daughter looked at Mary.

"Bah!" she said. "Maybe she has got a kind face, but I'm much prettier and my skin's whiter."

In the evening Mary finished the housework and decided to do some spinning. She sat down on the wooden bench, got out the silver distaff and golden spindle and began to spin. The thread that came out of the spindle was made of gold. As she worked, she looked into her silver distaff. She could see Phoenist there. He was alive and he was looking at her. Mary began to speak to him:

"Phoenist, Phoenist, bright falcon, why did you leave me alone? Why did you leave me to weep for you? It's my sisters, my cruel sisters, who shed your blood."

Just then the mistress's daughter came in. She stood by the door, watching and listening.

"Who is it you're weeping for?" she asked. "And what are you playing with?"

"I'm weeping for Phoenist the bright falcon," said Mary. "And I'm spinning a thread. I'm going to make Phoenist an embroidered towel, so he can wash his white face in the morning."

"Oh! Sell me your toy!" said the mistress's daughter. "Phoenist is my husband. I'll make him a towel myself."

72

Mary looked hard at the mistress's daughter. She stopped her golden spindle and said:

"I haven't got any toys; this is what I do my work with. And the silver distaff and golden spindle are not for sale. I was given them by a kind old woman."

The young mistress was very upset. She didn't want to let a golden spindle slip through her fingers.

"If they aren't for sale," she said, "let's do a swap. Give them to me and I'll give you a present."

"Yes!" said Mary. "Let me look at Phoenist the bright falcon just for a moment, with one eye."

The young mistress thought for a bit:

"All right then. Give me your toy."

She took Mary's silver distaff and golden spindle. She thought to herself:

"Why shouldn't she look at Phoenist for a few minutes? He won't come to any harm. And my mother and I will make lots of gold with this spindle."

Soon Phoenist the bright falcon came back from the sky. He turned into a handsome prince and sat down to have supper with his wife and mother-in-law.

The young mistress called Mary in so she could wait on them and see Phoenist. She came at once. She didn't take her eyes off Phoenist all the time she was in the room. And he just sat there without noticing her. He didn't recognize her: she was worn out from the journey and her face had changed with all she'd suffered for him. When they'd finished their supper, Phoenist got up and went to his room. He was very tired.

Mary said to the young mistress:

"There're a lot of flies about tonight. Let me go to Phoenist's room and keep them off him. Otherwise he won't be able to sleep."

"Why not?" said the mother.

73

The young mistress thought for a bit.

"All right, but she must wait a moment."

And then she went to her husband's room and gave him a sleeping potion. She thought that the maid might have some other toy she'd be willing to swap.

"Go along now," she said to Mary. "Go and keep the flies off my husband."

Mary went into Phoenist's room and forgot all about the flies. Her beloved was asleep and there was no way she could wake him up.

She looked and looked at him—she couldn't look long enough. She bent right down to him. She was breathing the same air as him. She whispered:

"Wake up, Phoenist, my bright falcon. It's me. I've found you. I've worn out three pairs of iron shoes and three iron staffs on the way, and I've eaten three loaves of stone."

But Phoenist didn't wake up. He didn't so much as open his eyes or say a single word.

Phoenist's wife, the young mistress, came in. She asked:

"Well, have you driven the flies away?"

"Yes, they've all flown out of the window."

"Well, then, it's time you went to bed."

The next day, when she'd done all the housework, Mary took her silver saucer and her golden egg. She span the egg round between her fingers—another egg rolled off the saucer. She span it round a second time—off rolled a third golden egg.

The young mistress had been watching.

"Oh! Have you got another toy? Sell it to me; or you can swap it for anything you like."

"I can't sell it," said Mary. "I was given it by a kind old woman. I can only give it to you. Take it!"

The young mistress took the silver saucer and the golden egg. She felt very pleased with herself.

"Mary, maybe there's something you'd like. You can ask for anything you want, you know."

"There's only one thing I want. Let me keep the flies off Phoenist again tonight."

"Of course," said the young mistress, and she thought to herself: "He won't come to any harm just from being looked at by a strange girl. I'll give him a sleeping potion and he won't even open his eyes. There might be some other toy I can get out of her."

Soon, Phoenist the bright falcon came back from the sky. He turned into a handsome prince and sat down to have supper with his family.

Phoenist's wife called Mary to wait on them. She laid the table and brought them their food, and she didn't once take her eyes off Phoenist. And Phoenist didn't recognize her. His heart didn't know her.

The young mistress gave him a sleeping potion again. When she'd put him to bed, she sent Mary along to keep the flies off him.

Mary went into Phoenist's room. She called his name and began to cry over him. She thought he'd wake up any moment, take one look at her and know her for his Mary. She called and called. She wiped the tears from her eyes so they wouldn't fall on his white face. And Phoenist slept. He didn't wake up. He didn't even open his eyes.

The third day, when Mary had finished the housework, she sat down on the wooden bench, took out her golden needle, and began to sew. She held the thimble in her hand and the golden needle sewed by itself.

As she worked, she said to herself:

"Sew away, sew away, beautiful cloth, embroider yourself for Phoenist the bright falcon. Be something for him to wonder at."

The young mistress was waiting nearby. When she heard

Mary talking, she came into the room and saw the golden needle and thimble sewing away by themselves. She was seized with greed and envy.

"Oh Mary, Mary, darling Mary! Sell me your toy or take anything you want in exchange for it. I've got a silver distaff and a golden spindle. I can spin thread and I can make cloth, but I haven't got a golden needle and thimble to embroider it with. If you don't want to swap it for anything, please sell it to me. I'll give you whatever you ask."

"No!" said Mary. "I can't sell my golden needle and thimble and I can't swap them for anything either. I was given them by the oldest, kindest, old woman. I can only give them to you."

The young mistress took the golden needle and thimble, but she hadn't got anything to give Mary. She said:

"If you want to, you can go along and keep the flies off my husband. You used to ask to do that."

"All right," said Mary.

At first the young mistress decided not to give Phoenist a sleeping potion, but then she changed her mind and put one in his drink. "Why let him look at a strange girl?" she thought to herself. "He'll be safer asleep."

Mary went into the room where Phoenist was sleeping. This time she could hardly bear it. She fell down by his bed and began to weep.

"Wake up, wake up, Phoenist my bright falcon. I've travelled the whole earth to find you. I've ground down three iron staffs, my feet have worn out three pairs of iron shoes, and I've swallowed three stone loaves. Wake up, my Phoenist! Have pity on me."

But Phoenist was asleep. He didn't feel anything. He couldn't hear Mary's voice.

Mary wept over him. She tried and tried to wake him up, but it was no good—the sleeping potion was too strong. But

76

then one of Mary's hot tears fell on his chest, and another one fell on his face. One burnt his heart, the other opened his eyes. He woke up.

"What's happened?" he said. "Something's burnt me."

"Phoenist, Phoenist my bright falcon," said Mary. "Wake up! It's me! I've come to you. I've searched and searched for you. I've worn iron shoes and iron staffs to nothing. Iron couldn't last out the journey. Only I could. And now I've been calling you for three nights, and all you've done is sleep. You haven't woken up or said a word to me."

At last Phoenist the bright falcon knew his Mary, his love. He was so happy he didn't know what to say. He just held her close to him, and kissed her.

When he came to himself, when he understood that his Mary was with him again, he said:

"Be a dove, my faithful love!"

Mary turned into a dove; Phoenist became a falcon.

They flew away into the night sky and flew side by side all through the night.

While they were flying, Mary said:

"Falcon, falcon, where are you flying to? Your wife will miss you."

Phoenist the bright falcon heard what she said and answered:

"I'm flying to your home, my love. A wife who sells her husband for a spindle, a saucer and a needle doesn't need a husband and won't miss him."

"What made you marry a wife like that?" asked Mary. "Was it against your will?"

"No, but it was against my fate, and without my love."

And they flew on, side by side.

They landed on the earth at sunrise. Mary looked round—there was her father's house, just as it always had been. Mary wanted to see her father and she turned back into a beautiful young woman. And Phoenist the bright falcon turned into a feather.

Mary took the feather, hid it between her breasts and went to her father.

"Greetings, daughter! My youngest, my beloved! I thought you had left the world. Thank you for coming home, for not forgetting your father. But where've you been all this time? Why didn't you come before?"

"Forgive me, Father. That's how it was fated."

"Well, fate's fate. Thank God you're back now."

She'd come back on the eve of a holiday. A big fair was opening in town. Her father was going there next morning. Her two sisters were going with him to buy themselves presents.

He asked Mary to come too.

"I'm worn out from my journeys, Father. Anyway, I haven't got anything to wear. Everyone will be wearing fine clothes at the fair."

"Mary, I'll buy you some fine clothes when we get there," said her father. "There'll be lots to choose from."

"You can wear some of our old clothes," said the older sisters. "We've got some we don't need."

"Thank you, sisters!" said Mary. "But your clothes are the wrong size. Anyway, I'd rather stay at home."

"Do as you please," said her father. "But what shall I buy for you at the fair? Tell me. Don't be cruel to your father."

"Dear Father, there isn't anything I want. I've got all I need. I didn't travel all that way for nothing."

The father rode off to the fair with his two older daughters. Mary took out her feather at once. It fell against the floor and turned into a handsome young prince, Phoenist. He was even more handsome than he'd been before. Mary gazed at him and was so happy she couldn't think what to say. Then Phoenist said:

78

"Don't look so surprised, Mary. I'm like that because you love me."

"I may look surprised," said Mary, "but you're always the same to me. I love you whatever you look like."

"Where's your father?"

"He's gone to the fair with my older sisters."

"Why didn't you go with them, Mary?"

"I've got Phoenist, my bright falcon. What do I need from the fair?"

"I don't need anything either, but I've grown rich with your love."

Phoenist turned away and whistled out of the window. At once there appeared a golden carriage, rich clothes and jewellery. They dressed up, sat down in the carriage, and the horses were off like lightning.

They got to the fair when it had only just opened. There were great heaps of all kinds of rich merchandise and costly goods, and the buyers were still on their way.

Phoenist bought everything there was in the market, all the food and all the clothes. He ordered it all to be taken by cart to the village where Mary's father lived. The only thing he didn't buy was the cartwheel grease. He left that on the stalls.

He wanted all the peasants who came to the fair to be guests at his wedding and to come as quickly as possible. To do that, they'd need to grease the wheels of their carts.

Phoenist and Mary set off back home. They went quickly. The horses could hardly breathe for the wind.

Half-way back, Mary saw her father and her older sisters. They were still on their way to the fair. Mary told them to go back home and come to her wedding with Phoenist the bright falcon.

In three days everyone who lived within a hundred miles had arrived. Phoenist and Mary were married. Their wedding was very splendid.

Our grandfathers and grandmothers all went to the wedding. They feasted a long time and drank toasts to the bride and groom. They'd have stayed till winter, but the wheat was already ripe in the fields and it was time to bring in the harvest. So the wedding ended.

The wedding ended. In time even the wedding feast was forgotten, but Mary's true loving heart is remembered for ever throughout all Russia.

Wool Over the Eyes

Once upon a time there was an old soldier called Ivan, who'd served in the army for twenty-five years. He'd always done his duty honourably, but he did like playing tricks on his comrades. He could say anything in the world and everyone would always believe it was true.

Now, a soldier may serve long hours, but even he's free part of the time and he wants to have some fun. He doesn't have a family, he doesn't have to think about board and lodging, so what does he do when he's finished sentry-duty? What do you think? He starts telling stories. The best story-teller of them all was Ivan.

Now Ivan was getting old. It was time he retired and went home to his family. But his home was somewhere far, far away and he'd forgotten about his family long ago.

"Well," he sighed, "I've spent all my life in the army. I've served for twenty-five years and I haven't once seen the Tsar. When I get back, my family are going to ask what he's like. What am I going to say?"

So Ivan went off to see the Tsar.

The Tsar of that land was Tsar Ajan. Tsar Ajan loved being told stories; he listened to some every evening and till then he never felt happy. He also liked telling stories and asking riddles himself; he liked it when people listened to him. He liked it even more when they believed his stories and couldn't guess his riddles.

In came Ivan.

"What do you want, fellow?" asked Ajan.

"I want to have a look at you," said Ivan. "I've served for twenty-five years and I haven't once seen the Tsar."

Tsar Ajan told him to sit down opposite him on a carved chair.

"Sit down! Have a good look! Sit down there, sit on my chair, sit till the devil takes you away by the hair."

Ivan sat down. He began to feel afraid of the Tsar. He thought he was probably a bit mad.

"Well, soldier, let me ask you a riddle!" said Ajan. "How big do you think the world is?"

Ivan looked very serious.

"Not that big, your highness. The sun goes round all of it in under twenty-five hours."

"True enough," said the Tsar. "And how far is it from the earth to the sky? Is it a long way?"

"It's not that far, your highness. If there's a knock up there, you can hear it down here."

The Tsar knew the old soldier was right and he didn't like it. He was afraid the old soldier was even cleverer than he was.

"And now tell me one more thing. How deep are the ocean depths?"

Ivan shook his head.

"No one knows that, your highness. My grandad was in the navy. He was drowned forty years ago. We haven't heard a word from him since."

Tsar Ajan realized he'd never beat the old soldier in

82

riddles. He had him given some money to set up house. Then he told him to sit down again and have some tea.

"Tell me a story now, soldier. Then you must go home."

Now a soldier never has any money at all and Ivan was very glad to be given some. He was getting bored at the Tsar's and anyway it wasn't really tea that he wanted.

"Let me go out for a drink, your highness. I've served in the army for twenty-five years. Now let me do as I like. I'll tell you a story afterwards."

Ivan left the Tsar's palace and went off to a pub. He stayed there for days and days. He drank away all the Tsar's money. All he had left was an old halfpenny. He drank that away too, but he still hadn't had his fill. He wanted more.

"Landlord, give us some more wine and a bite to eat."

The landlord was afraid of being cheated. He asked:

"Are you paying in gold or in silver?"

"In gold. Silver's too heavy for a soldier to carry around."

The landlord brought him some wine and some food, and then sat down opposite him.

"Where have you come from and where are you going to?" he asked. "And how are things with your family? Are they alive or dead?"

"I've just been at the Tsar's," said the soldier. "Where else? A soldier doesn't need a family. The whole world's his kin. Drink up, landlord, it's on me!"

The landlord and the old soldier drank together.

"I'll charge you a bit less," said the landlord. "You can have a discount."

"Drink up, landlord! And have something to eat! We can settle up later."

The landlord was used to being treated. He lived well and he liked a good talk.

"Tell me a story, soldier. Tell me about your life."

"What about it, landlord?"

"Anything you like, what people you've met, what countries you've seen."

"Well then, before I was a soldier, I was a bear and I lived in the forest. Now I'm a bear again and I'm on my way back to the forest."

The landlord was very worried when he heard this: it was his own pub and he had lots of goods there. A bear might make him lose money; how would he make a bear pay up?

"What!" he shouted. "You don't mean that, do you?"

"Of course I do!" said the soldier. "I'm a bear, and you're a bear too. Can't you see?"

The landlord was horrified. "How am I going to trade with anyone now I'm a bear," he thought.

He looked at the old soldier, pinched his own skin, and knew it was true: the old soldier was a bear; he was a bear himself.

"What can we do, soldier? Must we really go to the forest?"

"Not now, the hunters will get us. There'll be time enough later."

"Well, what shall we do now then? God, how unhappy I am! I'm a bear."

The old soldier stayed calm.

"We're all right. We can stay here for a bit. Why don't you give a feast? You can invite guests from all the villages. Bears can't be landlords and there's no point in just wasting your goods."

The landlord could see Ivan was right. He told his servants to go and invite the guests.

The guests were soon there—some who'd been invited, others who'd just heard about it. They ate and drank till there wasn't a drop or a crumb left. Then they took away all the knives, forks, plates, cups and glasses. They didn't think a bear would need that sort of thing.

Now the landlord didn't have anything left at all. He and the soldier climbed up on to their beds.

84

"What shall we do now?" asked the landlord.

"Tonight we'll run away to the forest. It's against the law for bears to live in towns and villages. We'll get fined."

Ivan woke up at midnight and said to the landlord:

"Come on, bear! Jump! You go first and I'll follow. Otherwise you'll get left behind."

The landlord got ready, jumped off the bed and fell flat on his face on the floor.

He lay there for a while till he came to. Then he saw what had happened—the pub was empty, his food had all been eaten, his wine had all been drunk, his plates and glasses had been taken away, and he himself was a landlord again, not a bear, though not so well off as he had been.

The landlord wanted to take the old soldier to court, but he hadn't got his address and he didn't know where to look for him. Anyway, people always welcome a soldier. No one would give him away.

The landlord made a complaint to Tsar Ajan. The Tsar summoned the landlord and asked him:

"What injury has the old soldier done you?"

"What do you mean, your highness?" said the landlord. "He turned me into a bear. I was a fool and believed him and he gave away everything I had. He gave away all my food and all my drink and took what he wanted himself. Then he disappeared."

Tsar Ajan laughed at the landlord.

"Be off with you!" he said. "Make yourself another fortune. There's no law against wit, and no profit in being stupid."

The Tsar immediately wanted the old soldier to tell him a story and make him believe things that weren't true. He thought to himself: "The old soldier can't be more clever than I am. I'm the Tsar. He won't pull the wool over my eyes. I'll have a good laugh at him."

The Tsar ordered the old soldier, Ivan, to be brought to him, wherever he was found.

Ivan heard the Tsar was calling him and came at once.

"Here I am, your highness," he said. "What do you want?"

The Tsar had the samovar brought in and offered Ivan some tea.

Ivan poured some tea into a silver cup, poured a little of it into the saucer, and sat down on a stool. He almost sat down on the carved chair, but he sat on the stool instead.

The Tsar said to him:

"You're clever, Ivan. I hear you turned a landlord into a bear. Can you do something like that to me?"

"Oh no, your highness! I'd be afraid."

"You needn't be afraid. I love a good story."

"All right then," said Ivan. "I'll tell you one. But what time is it, your highness?"

"What does that matter? It's about twelve."

"It'll start any minute!" said the old soldier.

After saying that, he suddenly shouted out:

"Water! Water, your majesty! The palace is flooding! Quick! We must escape! I'll tell the story later, somewhere dry."

The Tsar couldn't see the flood. He couldn't see any water anywhere. All he could see was that the old soldier was drowning. He was gasping for breath and stretching his mouth up for air.

"What's the matter, soldier?" he shouted. "Why are you drowning?"

Suddenly there's water climbing up his own legs. It reaches his chest. He can hardly breathe. There's water in his lungs, in his stomach. It's flowing into his guts.

"Help!" shouts the Tsar. "I'm drowning!"

Ivan grabs hold of the Tsar.

"Ajan, swim as hard as you can."

Ajan's swimming. In front of him there's a fish. Suddenly it turns round.

"Don't be frightened," it says. "Ajan, it's me, your soldier!"

The Tsar looks at himself: now he's a fish too.

He's very glad about that.

"Soldier," he shouts, "now we won't be drowned."

"We certainly won't!" answers Ivan-fish. "We'll live!"

They swim on. They swim out of the palace, into the open water. Suddenly Ivan-fish isn't there. The Tsar can hear him shouting somewhere to the left.

"Quick, Ajan, swim to the left! There's a net in front. You'll get fried."

The Tsar's not quick enough. He swims straight into the net. Ivan's there too.

"What are we going to do now, soldier?"

"We're going to die, your highness."

The Tsar wants to live. He struggles and struggles. He wants to jump out of the net, but it's too strong.

The fishermen pull in their catch. One of them grabs Ivan-fish, scrapes off his scales, and throws him into the pan. "Well," thinks the Tsar, "they won't scrape the scales off me in a hurry."

The other fisherman grabs the Tsar-fish, cuts off his head and throws it away, and tosses his body into the pan.

"But your highness, your excellency, where's your head?" says Ivan-fish.

Tsar Ajan wants to answer, "Well, where are your scales, you devil? Why didn't you save me?", but he remembers he hasn't got his head. He can't say a word.

The Tsar seized his head in his hands. Then he began to come to. He looked round: he was in his palace as he always had been; there wasn't a trace of water anywhere; the old soldier was sitting opposite him on a stool, drinking tea from a saucer.

"Ivan, was it you who was a fish just now?"

"Yes, your highness, who else?"

"And who was thinking, when I didn't have my head?"

"Me again. There wasn't anyone else."

Then the Tsar shouted out:

"Leave my kingdom at once! Let me never hear of you again! May your name be forgotten for ever."

The old soldier had to leave the palace. All he'd had to drink was a half-saucer of tea. The Tsar at once made a proclamation:

"Let no one in all my kingdom give hospitality to the old soldier Ivan."

Wherever Ivan went, people closed their doors to him. They wouldn't speak to him. All they said was:

"The Tsar forbade us to take you in."

For the first time in his life Ivan had made a mistake.

He went home to his family. They didn't want to know him.

"The Tsar forbade us to take you in," they said.

Ivan set off again. He didn't know what to do.

One evening he came to a hut and asked to stay the night there.

"Let me in, good man!"

"I'm not allowed to," the man answered. "Still, I might let you in if you tell me a story. You really do know how to tell stories, do you?"

Ivan thought for a moment.

"Yes, I think so."

The man let him in.

Ivan sat down and began to tell a story. At first his host listened without interest. "He'll just think up some tall story or other and then he'll expect to be fed," he thought to himself. After a while he smiled. Then he began to think. Soon he quite forgot who he was: he was a bandit; he was Tsar of the ocean; he was an idiot; or just a poor, very very wise, tramp. But really nothing was happening at all: there was just an old soldier sitting there, twitching his lips and muttering away.

When the story was over, the peasant came to and asked for another one. The soldier began again.

Soon it was nearly dawn and they still hadn't gone to bed. Ivan was telling his hundredth story and his host was sitting opposite him, crying tears of joy.

"That'll do!" said Ivan. "I'm only making things up. Why cry about nothing?"

"It's your stories," answered his host. "They're food for thought and a joy to the heart."

"But Tsar Ajan was angry with me," remembered Ivan.

"He ordered me to leave his kingdom and never again set foot in it."

"That's how it is," said the peasant. "The people's meat is the Tsar's poison."

Ivan got up and began to say goodbye to his host.

"Take anything of mine you want," said his host. "Nothing matters to me any more and you'll need something for the road."

"I've got everything I want already," said the soldier. "There isn't anything I need. But thank you!"

"Whatever it is you've got, I can't see it," said his host.

The old soldier smiled.

"So you think I'm penniless and yet you'll give me whatever I want. Well, I must have something to offer."

"You win," answered his host. "Well, God be with you! Come again, you'll always be welcome."

And Ivan set off again, wandering from village to village. Wherever he went, he only had to promise to tell a story and people would take him in for the night: a story's stronger than a Tsar. There was just one thing—if he began a story before supper, no one ever felt hungry and he didn't get anything to eat. He always had to ask for a bowl of soup first.

It was better like that. After all, you can't just live on stories, without any food.